Further praise for *Hint Fiction*

"The stories in Robert Swartwood's *Hint Fiction* have some serious velocity. Some explode, some needle, some bleed, and some give the reader room to dream. They're fun and addictive, like puzzles or haiku or candy. I've finished mine but I want more."

—Stewart O'Nan

*hint ficti

tion

hint fiction

An Anthology of Stories
in 25 Words or Fewer

Edited by
Robert Swartwood

 W. W. NORTON & COMPANY ✳ *New York London*

"Before Perseus" by Ben White. First published in *PicFic*, October 30, 2009.

"Claim" by Gwendolyn Joyce Mintz. First published in *Sexy Stranger*, February 2006, issue 4.

"Corrections & Clarifications" by Robert Swartwood. First published in *elimae*, October 2008.

"Found Wedged in the Side of a Desk Drawer in Paris, France, 23 December 1989" by Nick Mamatas. First published in *Lady Churchill's Rosebud Wristlet*, May 2003, issue 12.

"Free Enterprise" by Kelly Spitzer. First published in *elimae*, December 2007.

"The End or the Beginning" by James Frey © Big Jim Industries.

"The Mall" by Robley Wilson © Blue Garage Co.

"The Widow's First Year" by Joyce Carol Oates © Ontario Review, Inc.

For information about special discounts for bulk purchases, please contact
W. W. Norton Special Sales at specialsales@wwnorton.com or 800-233-4830

Manufacturing by Courier Westford
Book design by Judith Stagnitto Abbate/Abbate Design
Production manager: Devon Zahn

Library of Congress Cataloging-in-Publication Data

Hint fiction : an anthology of stories in 25 words
or fewer / edited by Robert Swartwood. — 1st ed.
p. cm.
ISBN 978-0-393-33846-1 (pbk.)
1. Short stories, American. 2. American fiction—21st century.
I. Swartwood, Robert.
PS648.S5H56 2010
813'.010806—dc22

2010016056

W. W. Norton & Company, Inc.
500 Fifth Avenue, New York, N.Y. 10110
www.wwnorton.com

W. W. Norton & Company Ltd.
Castle House, 75/76 Wells Street, London W1T 3QT

1 2 3 4 5 6 7 8 9 0

hint fiction (n): A story of 25 words or fewer that suggests a larger, more complex story.

contents

part 2
love & hate

part 3
this & that

My deepest thanks and
gratitude to John Cashman,
Amy Cherry, Gay Degani, Barry
Graham, Scott Miller, Stewart
O'Nan, Monica J. O'Rourke,
Holly Lyn Swartwood,

*

and each and every person
who has helped spread
the word of Hint Fiction
from the beginning.

"The king died and then the
queen died" is a story.

*

"The king died and then the
queen died of grief" is a plot.

— E. M. Forster,
Aspects of the Novel

introduction

For sale: baby shoes, never worn.

Although Ernest Hemingway is credited for creating the first "six-word story," some believe the story of its creation is a myth. The truth is there is no written account of those six words anywhere. They are, as one Hemingway scholar puts it, apocryphal.

Regardless, those six simple words have managed to change the landscape of the short story. There are anthologies and online magazines devoted to what is now referred to as the "six-word story." They are a testament to the paradox facing every writer: less is more.

I was inspired the first time I heard about the story. Not so much by the six words themselves—though they are quite impressive—but by the idea of writing a story in the fewest number of words possible. I knew each word had to be just right. I tried my hand at these stories but could never come up with anything I liked.

In the summer of 2007, I came across the corrections and clarifications section in a weekday copy of *USA Today*. It was a tiny paragraph buried in the corner of the page. It made me think about newspapers and articles and how one simple mistake, one overlooked error, could shake a city. Despite wanting never to think of that episode again, the newspaper would have no choice but to acknowledge the error. I suddenly had one of those writer's epiphanies. The result was a seventeen-word story aptly titled "Corrections & Clarifications," which was published in the October 2008 issue of the online journal *elimae*:

It was Fredrick Miller, not his murdered son Matthew, who was executed Monday night at Henshaw Prison.

At the time, I didn't know in what category to place that particular story. The hierarchy of fiction goes something like this: novel, novella, novelette, short story, sudden fiction, flash fiction, micro fiction, drabble, dribble. I'm sure there are more labels, many of which intersect at a certain word count. (At what point does sudden fiction become flash fiction? At what point does flash fiction become micro fiction?) Only two types have clear word distinctions: a drabble is a story of exactly one hundred words; a dribble, of fifty words.

What about my seventeen-word story, then? If it needed a label, how would it be classified?

Over the next couple of months I wrote a few more extremely short stories. Each happened to be one sentence, and so I referred to them as one-sentence stories. Yet even "one-sentence story" didn't quite do the form justice, as it's possible to write a one-hundred-word one-sentence story, or even a five-hundred-word one-sentence story.

In the spring of 2009, editor and writer Gay Degani put out a call for articles and essays about flash fiction for *Flash Fiction Chronicles*, the writing blog for the online magazine *Every Day Fiction*. I thought again about the Hemingway story and pitched an idea about how short a writer can make a story until it's no longer considered a story. What resulted was an essay I submitted a few weeks later titled "Hint Fiction: When Flash Fiction Becomes Just Too Flashy."

In the essay, I proposed that the very best storytelling was the kind where the writer and reader meet halfway, the writer only painting fifty percent of the picture and forcing the reader to fill in the rest. That way, the reader truly becomes engaged in the process.

Very, very, very short stories, however, like Hemingway's, do not meet the writer halfway. In fact, they rarely meet the reader a tenth of the way. A reader would be lucky if he or she were to get one percent of the story. And that's why I called it Hint Fiction—because the reader is only given a *hint* of a much larger, more complex story.

The essay was published, and to help promote the idea, I hosted a Hint Fiction Contest at my blog. I encouraged writers to submit up to two stories of twenty-five words or fewer. The grand prize was a $25 gift certificate for Amazon.com. Novelist Stewart O'Nan was even kind enough to act as the final judge. It was going to be a fun little contest, nothing more, with maybe a handful of entries.

Over the course of a week and a half, the concept of Hint Fiction spread rapidly across the Internet. Blog after blog picked it up. Entries began to stream in, so much so that by the time the contest closed, more than two hundred entries had been submitted. Of those two hundred entries, twenty finalists were chosen by Gay Degani and me, and those were sent to Stewart, who made his top picks (first place: "House Hunting" by Gary A. Braunbeck; second place: "Departure" by Donora Hillard; third place: "Progress" by Joe Schreiber). All twenty stories can be found in this book.

At the start of this project, it was important to create a definition of what Hint Fiction was. Most importantly, I didn't want people to think it was just twenty-five words or fewer written down on a page. Each story had to do something special. In the end I came up with the thesis that a story of twenty-five words or fewer can have as much impact as a story of twenty-five hundred words or longer.

As you can imagine, there was resistance. You see, there is a school of thought that doesn't appreciate these very, very, very short stories. These people don't even see them as stories. For them, these stories contain no beginning, no middle, no end. No protagonist, no conflict. Also, predictably, other people complained about the length. How can something so brief be taken seriously? If a story is that short, couldn't *anyone* be called a writer?

It's my belief that the length of a story does not determine the credentials of a writer. After all, at what point does a story stop being a story? It's always a slippery slope when people begin placing limitations on art, and to immediately dismiss one form because of its length is simply shortsighted.

For me, a story should do four basic things: obviously it should tell a story; it should be entertaining; it should be thought-provoking; and, if done well enough, it should invoke an emotional response.

Now, if those four basic principles can be applied to a story of twenty-five hundred words, why can't they be applied to an even shorter story?

When I put out a call for submissions for

this book, I received more than twenty-four hundred stories. A majority read as if they were first sentences of a much larger work. Others read like random thoughts, or even incomplete thoughts. A few painted beautiful pictures and nothing else. Still others were complete stories—beginning, middle, end—all wrapped up in twenty-five words or fewer: an impressive feat, but ultimately even those were not the stories I was looking for.

Hint Fiction should not be complete by it having a beginning, middle, and end. Instead it should be complete by standing by itself as its own little world. The stories found within this book may look small and insignificant, but each is powerful in its own special way.

There are some who will see the popularity of these stories as an indication of our short attention spans. Yes, people have short attention spans nowadays, but should that be any reason to disregard or dismiss Hint Fiction or other short forms? If anything, Hint Fiction is an exercise in brevity, with the writer trying to affect the reader in as few words as possible.

There's a reason why Hemingway's story has survived so long and become so popular. It seems very, very, very short stories speak to something deep inside readers. Guatemalan writer Augusto Monterroso, now deceased, is credited with writing one of the world's shortest stories: "The Dinosaur," published in his 1959 short story collection *Obras completas (y otros cuentos)*. Fredric Brown, a science fiction writer, is well known for his story "Knock." It begins with a two-sentence story that then grows into a much larger story. What's interesting is that over the years the rest of the story has been pretty much forgotten and only those two sentences have survived. American author Lydia Davis—whose 2007 short story collection *Varieties of Disturbance* was a finalist for the National Book Award—is widely known for writing stories that are no longer than a sentence or two. In this book you will find stories by award-winning and bestselling authors such as

Stephen Dunn, James Frey, Ha Jin, Joyce Carol Oates, and Peter Straub, who traditionally conjure up much larger works, alongside new writers whose first published fiction may be shorter than their name and address.

Hint Fiction sometimes speaks to our hearts, and at other times manages to catch us off guard. I could go in-depth about every story in this book, but I'll let the stories speak for themselves, as all good fiction should.

part 1
life & death

joe r. lansdale

They buried him deep.
Again.

kevin hosey

CURE

Triumphant, Dr. Masuyo held the
frail child. After years, he finally had a cure.
Outside, the sun warmed Hiroshima. And
then he saw the flash.

blake crouch

THE NEWTON BOYS' LAST PHOTOGRAPH

Their sunglasses reflect the backpack on the raft which will hold the camera, which will hold the film, which will hold this eerie, smiling moment.

hannah craig

NOT WAVING

"What's he doing out there?"
Marnie asked.

We were sick of the lake, sunburned, and
wanted to go home.

I muttered, "I have no idea."

charles gramlich

IN A PLACE OF LIGHT
AND REASON

Sarah watched her son
through the window, as
he stood in the garden
and bloomed roses with
his hands.

bob thurber

SHIPWRECKED

After we buried the captain,
we salvaged the Victrola. It worked, though
the mahogany was ruined. Half of us put on
dresses. And we danced.

jane hammons

THE LAND WITH NO AIR

Grandpa breathes from a tank. He's selling the ranch because he doesn't have any air.

Mama says, I'm your heir.

He says, You're a girl.

michael martone

IN THE TALLADEGA
NATIONAL FOREST

Looking for the body, we found
hundreds of burned-out lightbulbs in a
clearing. Found four bodies, but not the body
we were looking for.

ben jahn

KENNY &
SON

We found him in a motel a mile north of San
Quentin. He had the Gideon open on the
nightstand so the boy would see.

stace budzko

WHY I DON'T KEEP
A DAILY PLANNER

Written on his calendar on the day of my father's death, these words: *Call son*.

will panzo

THE MAN OF TOMORROW OR MAYBE YOU'VE HEARD THIS ONE BEFORE, BUT YOU'VE NEVER HEARD IT LIKE THIS

Dying planet. A boy, a rocket, a last hope. Kansas cornfield crash landing. Ma finds it sleeping in the crater. Pa fetches the shotgun.

barry napier

When they opened the cadaver, they found a house. A couple argued inside. There was rhythm to their words, like the beating of a heart.

kirsten beachy

FERTILITY

My Muscovy duck hatched seventeen
ducklings—along with four chicks from eggs the
hens snuck into her nest.

I'm still waiting.

jennifer haddock

PREGNANCY TEST

A drop of pee. An unanswered prayer. The second pink line draws one childhood to an end as another begins.

jake thomas

CHILDREN

He took her out for a picnic to discuss what they wanted to do about it. "You want Bud Light or O'Doul's?" he asked her.

shanna germain

NICK OF TIME

I press my feet into the OB/GYN
stirrups and realize I'm wearing my Santa
socks. Green and red with fat Santas eating
cookies. It's June.

madeline mora-summonte

THE EMPTY NEST

My wife curls toward me,
a comma forcing a
pause. Her body is hers.
Again. The emptiness
settles between us. We
listen to it breathe.

jamie felton

A SNAP DECISION

Her finger tapped against her teeth. "I don't think it's going to work." He sank slowly underneath the surface. She could still see his eyelashes.

jack ketchum

THAT MOMENT

The old cat blinked once,
focused. Then was lost to her forever.

BIGGER THAN IT LOOKS

Her eyes moved to the shovel tapping nervously against his toe, then down to her hands. "Such a small hole. It's just— so small."

brian crawford

THE DAY AFTER

He started to put the cover back on the pool
but stopped. What was the point? He had
needed it yesterday.

samuel rippey

CIVILIAN

Ruby burned every one of her swimsuits after one use. I abhorred the waste but understood her point. "Habit," she said. "After the first bomb."

daniel a. olivas

BETTER THAN DIVORCE

The bull terrier watched the car fishtail and then straighten as it sped away. The dog turned, looked down, and gently licked his master's forehead.

rose rappoport moss

MURDER FOR HIRE

In court he said Sparkle, his daughter-in-law and family's shame, used to laugh like water in sunshine. How could he have hurt her himself?

j. a. konrath

DONOR

Miller watched from his hospital bed as the brakes on his son's Indy-racer failed. When they pulled his lifeless body from the wreck, Miller smiled.

mercedes m. yardley

PUBLIC MOURNING

It was Shark Week again. She flipped the TV
off. She couldn't bear to watch him die one
more time.

nicky drayden

PUSHOVER

He shoves me aside to get a better view. I never fight back. He's worn me down, weaker than that railing at the canyon's rim.

f. paul wilson

PRANKSTERS

Bad enough what they did to the flowers, but the cat was the last straw. Nine in the magazine. That oughta do.

max barry

BLIND DATE

She walks in and heads turn. I'm stunned. This is my setup? She looks sixteen. Course, it's hard to tell, through the scope.

benjamin percy

IMPACT

The boy would never forget the expression on his sister's face when he pulled the trigger of the rifle he thought unloaded.

eric hsu

AN IMPROMPTU ROBBERY

The pen, which was attached to the bank counter, did not go all the way through his throat.

janet e. gardner

His life did not flash before his eyes, but his mouth filled with the taste, perfectly remembered from childhood, of lemon buttercream frosting.

camille esses

PEANUT BUTTER

He was allergic. She
pretended not to know.

kathleen a. ryan

PLAYING WITH MATCHES

Dragging the burning mattress down the stairs, she lit the house on fire. The kids cowered behind the dresser, where the firemen later found them.

sophie playle

FOR HER OWN
SAFETY

She was allowed photographs.
She ran her fingertips around frames, tears
welling. But she didn't lament; she just wished
they hadn't removed the glass.

john minichillo

THE STRICT PROFESSOR

A card in the mailbox:
"Withdrawal: student deceased." She
remembers the name, the only essay
in the stack she'll really read.

amber whitley

ONE MORE TOAST

Light shimmers off vodka and stale sweat; a
baby cries in the background. "*Na zdorovye*." At
the door, a knock.

michael kelly

3000 GRAY BALLOONS IN A BRIGHT BLUE SKY

That morning he was weightless. At the station, he smelled ash. Later, reaching for dust-caked limbs, he floated away, squinting against the sky's brilliance.

l. r. bonehill

CULL

There had been rumors from the North for months. None of us believed it, until one night we started to kill our children too.

peter straub

THE ENDLESS MYSTERY

When, on his deathbed, he last saw her, she had not aged by so much as a day.

joyce carol oates

THE WIDOW'S FIRST
YEAR

"I kept myself alive."

katrina robinson

VISITING HOURS

She placed her hand over his and pressed the pen to paper. The signature looked shaky, but it should be enough.

edith pearlman

GOLDEN YEARS

She: Macular. He: Parkinson's. She pushing,
he directing, they get down the ramp, across
the grass, through the gate. The wheels roll
riverwards.

james frey

THE END OR THE BEGINNING

Across the river.

The city.

Was just waking.

When I saw the flash.

Heard the noise.

Felt the shockwave.

Everything disappeared.

Except the blooming cloud.

j. matthew zoss

HOUSTON, WE HAVE
A PROBLEM

I'm sorry, but there's not enough air in here for everyone. I'll tell them you were a hero.

part 2
love & hate

nick arvin

KNOCK KNOCK
JOKE

My father, standing at the sink with
white sleeves rolled, says, "Knock knock."

I say, "Who's there?"

"She loves."

"She loves who?"

He says, "Exactly."

ben white

BEFORE PERSEUS

Medusa heaves his rigid stone form off herself
and cries granite tears. The hat wasn't enough,
she thinks. I need some blindfolds.

robley wilson

THE MALL

What he liked best
about the affair was
not the shopping, but
parting the tissue wrap
to remove the clothing
that had first enticed
her.

min jin lee

IN COMMON

"When do you read?" Helene asked the man.

"Before bed."

"Your wife?"

"She doesn't."

He took out a pen, and Helene took off
her glasses.

jason jordan

TAKE IT OFF

Without her knowing, Mark posted the video. A million views meant he had to show it to her before someone else did.

noel sloboda

DIVORCE PAPERS

When she gave me the homemade coupons, she insisted they were just for fun: one for a night of lovemaking, one for breakfast in bed.

don lee

TRUST

At the party, he tells her he's a painter,
meaning of houses. She misunderstands,
assumes he's an artist. Harmless, he thinks.

jonathan carroll

FOOLED AGAIN

She was like certain colognes: they smell
beautiful at first, but then the aroma disappears
in half an hour.

ken bruen

He took her by surprise
and she, she took him
for all he was worth.

brendan o'brien

WAITING

I ask Ben to hurry up, finish.
Sadly he is much like his father. I grind molars,
my one horrible habit. Well, one of them.

kirk curnutt

AFTERGLOW

He fumbled across the pillow to stroke his
wife's shoulder.

"Ailie—you sleeping already?"

"That's Tracy," answered a voice at his back.
"I'm over here."

david joseph

POLYGAMY

I miss her more than
the others.

joe schreiber

PROGRESS

After seventeen days she finally broke down
and called him "Daddy."

jason rice

PHILIP

The sound of breaking glass got Philip out of bed, and then he remembered he was no longer in love with his wife.

john cashman

ONE MONTH TOO SOON

Penelope was wakened by the cheers from the agora. She turned to the man in her bed and whispered, "What have I done?"

robin hollis

CHASTE

I always thought it would hurt more but I kind of liked it. He hoped I would. And technically I'm still a virgin. Amen.

christina kopp

BLESSING

As he traced the cross on her husband's
forehead, then hers, the priest felt both pain
and pleasure. He would never touch her again.

gay degani

BETRAYAL

Her husband left because of guilt. Not because of anything he had done, but because of what had been done to her by her father.

ann harleman

REUNION

You wear a shawl of moonlight, and my mouth
where your breast used to be.

"We waited too long," you say.

"Not quite."

james burt

RAPUNZEL

The boys waited below the tower-block for the paper planes. They fought over them, to be the one to carry them back to her.

christoffer molnar

JERMAINE'S POSTSCRIPT TO HIS SEVENTH-GRADE POEM ASSIGNMENT

"Ms. Tyler, the girl part was about Shantell. Please don't tell anyone."

bruce harris

Ninth inning. Bases loaded. Two out. Cody looks at a called third strike. He's petrified to look at his father.

k. j. maas

SILENCE

She wondered what it was like in his silent
world, and wished she could tell him. Instead,
she traced his eyebrows with her fingertips.

jenn alandy

CHECKING IN

His wife calls while we are in the hotel room.
"Yeah, I'm enjoying my time without the kids,"
he says. I stare at my feet.

sue williams

TRYST

"Shh," she whispers, leading you up. The stairs heave like an old man's groans. She smells of sex already. "I care about him, see?"

tess gerritsen

They are now grown
up, the children I
abandoned to be with
you. They hate me.
But not nearly as much
as I hate you.

adam-troy castro

CHANCE MEETING AT THE INSURANCE OFFICE

He had a fat neck, predatorial eyes, and a smirk of cruel recognition. "Yes," I said, without any pleasure. "I do remember you from high school."

j. j. steinfeld

THE EXACT COST OF THE YOUNG COUPLE'S FORTHCOMING WEDDING

Before their wedding, Gino revealed he was adopted. Eugenia admitted she was adopted too.

I was a twin, Gino added.

Eugenia said, So was I.

ENGAGEMENT

The dry cleaner offers
me a discount on the
wedding dress that's
been hanging in his
window for six months.

chris compson

PROCESSIONAL

The flowers did not wilt in the heat. She looked lovely. Each mother cried, perhaps noticing her teeth, clenched too tight, like jail bars.

val gryphin

INSOMNIA

Sleeping Beauty never minded the spindle prick. It was the wake-up kiss she hated.

marcus sakey

THE TIME BEFORE THE LAST

He held her crepe-paper hand and summoned an autumn day, sepia and smoke, and dancing, and music that sounded nothing like the beeping of machines.

david miller

THE PASSWORD

He thinks about using her name as the
password. No. He looks away from the screen.
Looks back. Swallows. Types: one_more_river
_song.

samuel j. baldwin

She flew from Savannah to Phoenix. Now she's crying in the bathroom. All I can think is: *The bathroom's moldy—I need to clean more*.

douglas clegg

COLD, COLD HEART

Alan felt a stab of sexual jealousy when another
med student claimed Jonathan first, who—
beautiful and indifferent—lay upon the table.

lewis manalo

MY MOTHER'S KISSES

Taking Greta's nipple in his teeth, he fought
to keep the image of his older sister from his
mind.

agnieszka stachura

TEMPTATION

They play hide-and-seek every Saturday, and every Saturday I smoke a Marlboro and watch them from the other side of the chain-link fence.

sarah lyons

THE DATE

How could he admit that this was not, actually, the first time he had seen Claudia's scar? He couldn't. He would have to feign surprise.

john connors

PILLOW TALK

"Smile for me and I'll stop."

She looked away.

"One smile. Please."

She refused.

"Stop crying."

She couldn't.

gregg hurwitz

DAMAGE

She lowered the toilet lid and sat, wiping the blood on the insides of her thighs. At the door came a distressed banging.

bill graffius

A CORPOREAL SUNRISE

As sunlight streamed through the window
he marveled at the bloodstained sheets,
remembering the tacit understanding that in
the morning she would be gone.

rachel lopez

DISCOVERY

While she retched in the guest bathroom,
he stood beside her, naked and ridiculous.

I said, "Get up, sweetheart. You're going
home."

ryan w. bradley

AFTER HE LEFT, BEFORE THE EXULTATION

Susan turned from the road, walked to the house, and spent the evening reassembling the words that had passed from his lips to her ear.

randall brown

The autistic boy wanted
to pet *her* head. She
made herself stay, as
if he rubbed out the
world—and she, the
only thing left.

jessa slade

THE OTHER SIDE OF THE DOOR

She waited, quietly, as a lady should.
Around her feet, dust settled soft as death.
He'd chosen the tiger. As they always did.

merrilee faber

LOVE IS FOREVER

We came around the corner and there they were: young lovers, hands clasped. I drew the outline, Joe directed the crowd.

part 3
this & that

frank byrns

TALKING OF MICHELANGELO

"Call me Ishmael."

She stared blankly, then grinned. "I'm going to hit the keg—need a refill?"

Ish sighed. No one reads anymore.

david joseph

MEIN FÜHRER

By now I've burned
more pages than
I've read.

robin rozanski

TONGUE

Excuse me?

Tongue, he repeated. Tongue the notes.

She replayed the étude. The result was so
obvious it seemed obscene. Unnecessary.
An excess of separation.

gwendolyn joyce mintz

CLAIM

The school bus picks
us up first so we claim
the back seats. Make the
white kids sit up front.

david hirsch

PAROLING CHARLES MANSON

Writing it on the board to reinforce the concept of "oxymoron," I thought *What's an oxymoron?* would be their first question. It was the second.

jeremy d. brooks

SHOW AND TELL

Each bubble-wrap cell was injected with red water. Bobbie rolled on it, frantic, screaming: *"Pop, pop, shriek!"*

"Well," said Teacher, "someone had an interesting summer."

ha jin

IDEAL

The boy dreams of
becoming a panda,
who makes money
by meeting visitors.
For such a pampered
celebrity, even a
girlfriend is provided.

stephen dunn

THE AMPUTEE

Wes returned in his wheelchair to where he'd been mugged, dollar bills sticking out of his pockets, a .38 under his folded pant leg.

kelly spitzer

FREE
ENTERPRISE

Retail. Thirty-nine hours a week for
eighteen years, she says, proud. Like she's
a survivor of rape and she knows it.

yvonne brockwell

KNIVES AND MEN

Whenever a knife hit the floor, a man would come to the house. She thinks about dropping knives. Klink. Klank. Clunk. That oughta do.

DICKIE

Everyone in town went to the same
gynecologist, Dickie. Even Dickie's sister went
to Dickie. No one thought this was strange
except for the out-of-towners.

shanna germain

NOAH'S DAUGHTER

"Can't you count? I said two of each. This"—
he shook the squirming fluff of black and white
in front of her—"is three."

jenifer rosenberg

PLAINCLOTHES

The bust of a lifetime, now falling apart because one small child—his son—had placed a happy face sticker on his jacket.

mabel yu

WITNESS

He would remember
hot oil staining the
white paper bag with
grease butterflies. But
not the argument, the
license plate, the single
opal earring.

andrea slye

LUCKY

She fingered the leash on the nail at the bottom of the stairs. What did Daddy need a leash for? They didn't own a dog.

stephen dunn

MIDNIGHT IN THE
EVERGLADES

"You dumb fuck. You
pathetic, dumb fuck."

frank byrns

ASSIMILATION

My name is Phuc. People call me John.

david erlewine

TELLING

At eighty-five, Mort decided to talk about his covert stutter. He told orderlies, residents, nurses, visitors. He wanted a wife or child to tell.

danielle combs

HOPE

The little girl stretched up on her tiptoes as her mother scratched her height into the wall, reaching for the emptiness above her crown.

stuart dybek

RANSOM

Broke and desperate, I kidnapped myself.

Ransom notes were sent to interested parties.
Later, I sent hair and fingernails, too.

They insisted on an ear.

ty miller

A DIGNIFIED PURPOSE

She loved to steal spoons. She didn't need them; she just enjoyed having a hundred tiny silver mirrors to see what no one else could.

marshall ryan maresca

REMINDER

The tiny stain never came out. No one else would notice, but he always knew. They were his favorite pants.

roxane gay

THE COPPER MINER'S
SAD SAD SONG

He took up drinking after the mine closed, still
needed something dark to crawl down into.
Difference was now, he took us down with him.

nada faris

TWELVE YEARS OF
FAMILY SECRETS

She shows them the DNA test result
as if it were a diploma. My mother doesn't clap
like the rest.

jess row

A QUIET
AMERICAN

He realized, taking a long swig from his beer,
that no one had told him whether swallowing
the octopus was guaranteed to kill it.

jack kilborn

CHUCK

Flight attendant Sherri was always quick to offer airsick bags. Reverse-bulimia, though a disgusting disease, was bearable for her when the meals were fresh.

gary a. braunbeck

HOUSE HUNTING

The fence is tall. Good.
The mother is typical white trash, too loud.
But the kids . . . they seem frightened and
quiet. Good. Easier that way.

natalie mcnabb

They call him the Cigarette Nazi of Sand Lake Store. When the kids finish their cigarettes, he watches them slip the butts into denim pockets.

sarah p. miller

WORKING FOR MOM

It was filed under Business Receipts, but what kind of meeting took place in the champagne suite? She reminded herself: assistant first, daughter second.

jade walker

SLEEP DEPRIVATION

He'd told them the truth. He was just a messenger. He didn't know anything. His legs and back ached, but still they made him stand.

ron carlson

Our job was to
lubricate the time
machine and keep it
oiled, but man, we just
now found out we're
being paid by the hour.

nick mamatas

FOUND WEDGED IN THE
SIDE OF A DESK DRAWER
IN PARIS, FRANCE,
23 DECEMBER 1989

```
BECKETT / WAITING     p. 49


GODOT enters, stage left.
```

william j. brazill

ART ALONE ENDURES

The Art League had a competition for artists to depict the future. By accident Bogdan included a blank canvas among his submissions. It won.

donora hillard

DEPARTURE

The terminal is unkind. You watch me go
through security. In six months, you'll say,
"Tell me about the nightmare," and I promise
I will.

about the authors

Jenn Alandy is twenty-seven, has two jobs, one lover (Saul), zero passport stamps, one University of California, Irvine, BA, one full brother (Joshsta), three scars, one hundred dreams.

Nick Arvin is the author of *In the Electric Eden* and *Articles of War*. His new novel, *The Reconstructionist*, will be out in 2011.

Samuel J. Baldwin is an outdoors writer in Casper, Wyoming. He fly-fishes with an unbecoming fervor, and loves Alex, cheap beer, and mystery novels.

Max Barry is the author of the novels *Syrup*, *Jennifer Government*, and *Company*. He lives in Melbourne, Australia, and blogs at http://max barry.com.

Kirsten Beachy lives in the Shenandoah Valley. She writes about poultry and Mennonite martyrs; her work appears in *Shenandoah*, *Relief*, the *Tusculum Review*, and elsewhere.

L. R. Bonehill never meant to hurt anyone all those years ago; he just wanted to play, that's all.

Ryan W. Bradley has fronted a punk band, done construction in the Arctic Circle, and now manages an independent children's bookstore.

Gary A. Braunbeck has published ten novels and ten short story collections. He has won five Bram Stoker Awards and an International Horror Guild Award.

William J. Brazill lives in Virginia on the banks of the Potomac River, where he writes fiction and watches the water flow by.

Yvonne Brockwell is a middle-aged single parent (widowed) who has been laid off for over a year from a job she resented. Hallelujah.

Jeremy D. Brooks is a fiction writer, journalist, poet, family guy, and spooky prop maker. Visit him at www.jeremydbrooks.com.

Randall Brown directs and teaches at Rosemont College's MFA of Creative Writing Program. He is the author of the award-winning flash collection *Mad to Live*.

Ken Bruen is the author of twenty-six published novels. He has won ten awards for the Jack Taylor series, and has a PhD in metaphysics.

Stace Budzko has published in *Night Train, Field Guide to Flash Fiction, Flash Fiction Forward, Brevity/Echo, Quick Fiction, SmokeLong, Long Story Short,* and *Southeast Review.*

James Burt was always advised to write what he knew, but suspects people aren't all that interested in computer programming. He makes things up instead.

Frank Byrns is the editor of *A Thousand Faces, the Quarterly Journal of Superhuman Fiction.* Visit him at www.frankbyrns.com.

Ron Carlson's most recent book is *The Signal.* He teaches at the University of California, Irvine.

Jonathan Carroll is the author of sixteen books. He lives in Vienna, Austria.

John Cashman, a graduate of Boston College, is a longtime high school English teacher presently living in Lititz, Pennsylvania.

Adam-Troy Castro's novels include *Emissaries from the Dead* and *The Third Claw of God*. He lives in Miami with his wife, Judi.

Douglas Clegg is the author of several works of fiction, including *Isis*, *Neverland*, *The Priest of Blood*, and others. He lives in New England.

Danielle Combs was born in Stockton, California, and moved to Lodi in the first grade. She will be graduating from Lodi High this year.

Chris Compson's work has appeared most recently in *Louisiana Literature* and *Paradigm*. He lives outside Syracuse, New York, where he teaches English.

John Connors lives in Pennsylvania with his wife, Jaime. He began submitting fiction for publication in 2008. This is his first professional sale.

Hannah Craig's work has recently appeared in *Smartish Pace*, *Tampa Review*, and *Northwest Review*. She lives in Pittsburgh, Pennsylvania.

Brian Crawford lives in San Francisco. He writes a blog called *The Leaf Blower* (http://the leafblower.blogspot.com), about quitting his biotechnology job to write a novel.

Blake Crouch's latest novel is *Abandon*. His short fiction has appeared in *Ellery Queen* and numerous anthologies. His Web site is www.blake crouch.com.

Kirk Curnutt's books include the novels *Dixie Noir* (2009) and *Breathing Out the Ghost* (2008). He lives and writes in Montgomery, Alabama.

Tara Deal is a writer and editor in New York City. Visit her at www.taradeal.com.

Gay Degani has published short stories online and in print, including four anthologies. She is currently working on a mystery novel. Find her at www.gaydegani.com.

Nicky Drayden is a systems analyst who'd rather spend her time working with prose than code. She resides in Austin, Texas.

Stephen Dunn is the author of fourteen books of poems, including *Different Hours*, which won the Pulitzer Prize. He lives in Frostburg, Maryland.

Stuart Dybek's most recent books are *I Sailed with Magellan* (fiction) and *Streets in Their Own Ink* (poems). He is Writer in Residence at Northwestern University.

David Erlewine's flash fiction appears in places like *FRiGG*, *Thieves Jargon*, and *The Pedestal*. He edits flash for *JMWW*. Visit his blog at www.whizbyfiction.blogspot.com.

Camille Esses currently attends Brooklyn College and is majoring in creative writing.

Merrilee Faber lives in the Far West, surrounded by sand and scrub. Writer, birder, geek. Loves sunshine, loathes flies.

Nada Faris has a BA in English Literature from Kuwait University and is currently studying at its MA Program of Comparative Literature.

Jamie Felton's first published work is very small, like a button or a tooth. She hopes to write and play music until she can't anymore.

James Frey is from Cleveland, Ohio. His work is published in thirty-five languages.

Janet E. Gardner is a student in the Stone-coast MFA program in fiction. She lives and writes on Cape Cod.

Roxane Gay is the associate editor of *PANK*. She can be found online at http://www.roxane gay.com.

Shanna Germain tries to say as much as possible with as few words as possible; thus, writing novels kicks her ass. Visit her at http://yearof thebooks.wordpress.com.

Tess Gerritsen is the internationally bestselling author of more than a dozen thriller novels, including the Jane Rizzoli crime series. She lives in Maine.

Bill Graffius, the college-educated son of a Pittsburgh millworker, looks for the exceptional in the ordinary, seeking to give it a voice through poetry.

Charles Gramlich has sold four novels, numerous short stories, and a book on writing entitled *Write with Fire*. Visit his blog at http://charlesgramlich.blogspot.com.

Val Gryphin lives in the Green Mountains, and has been published in several online and print journals. Her online home is http://val gryphin.com.

Jennifer Haddock is a writer and therapist from Baltimore. Previous publications include self-help articles and a work of fiction in *6S* (McEvily, 2008).

Jane Hammons teaches writing at the University of California, Berkeley, and writes fiction, essays, magazine articles, and sometimes poetry. Short and long.

Ann Harleman is the author of two story collections—*Happiness* and *Thoreau's Laundry*—and two novels—*Bitter Lake* and *The Year She Disappeared*.

Bruce Harris lives and works in New Jersey. His fiction has appeared in *The First Line*, *elimae*, *BULL*, and *Pine Tree Mysteries*.

Donora Hillard is the author of the forthcoming poetry collection *Theology of the Body* and has been an instructor of writing at Penn State University.

David Hirsch was raised in Erie, Pennsylvania, but taught English in Cleveland, Ohio. Now retired, he lives in Summerville, South Carolina, with his wife, Helen.

Robin Hollis is a native Texan. She has a degree in political science and enjoys reading and writing short fiction.

Kevin Hosey has had stories published by Pocket Books. His first novel is currently braving the editorial gauntlet at another publisher. Visit him at www.kevinhosey.net.

Eric Hsu is, among other things, a writer hailing from the great state of New Jersey.

Gregg Hurwitz is the internationally bestselling, critically acclaimed author of ten thrillers, most recently *They're Watching*. He also writes screenplays, and comics for Marvel.

Ben Jahn's fiction has appeared in several literary journals. He lives in the San Francisco Bay Area.

Ha Jin has published thirteen books in English. His work has been translated into more than thirty languages.

Jason Jordan holds an MFA from Chatham University. Visit his blog at www.poweringthe devilscircus.blogspot.com.

David Joseph is a California-born, New Jersey–raised writer and musician.

Michael Kelly's work can be found in *Post-scripts*, *Supernatural Tales*, and *Tesseracts 13*.

Jack Ketchum is the author of twelve novels, four of which have been recently filmed, and five collections of short fiction. He lives with cats.

Jack Kilborn: See bio for J. A. Konrath.

J. A. Konrath has written fourteen novels and more than seventy short stories. He also writes as Jack Kilborn and Joe Kimball. Visit him at www.jakonrath.com.

Christina Kopp is a writer and teacher who lives in Pennsylvania with her husband, two cats, and a groundhog named Frankie.

Minter Krotzer lives in Philadelphia, where she is at work on her first book, a collection of short nonfiction entitled *Firsts*.

Joe R. Lansdale is the author of thirty-five novels, twenty-one short story collections, and has won numerous awards for his fiction. He lives in Nacogdoches, Texas.

Don Lee is the author of the novels *Wrack and Ruin* and *Country of Origin* and the story collection *Yellow*. He teaches at Temple University.

Min Jin Lee's novel *Free Food for Millionaires* was chosen as one of the Top 10 Books of the Year in the *New York Times*, NPR's *Fresh Air*, and *USA Today*.

Rachel Lopez is an MFA student in the Creative Writing and Environment program at Iowa State University, with a focus on impoverished urban spaces.

Sarah Lyons lives in Austin, Texas, with various biting pets.

K. J. Maas is an almost-lifelong resident of Delaware, and owes it all to Mom, Dad, and family.

Nick Mamatas is the author of two novels, *Under My Roof* and *Move Under Ground*, and of the short story collection *You Might Sleep* . . .

Lewis Manalo's wife asked him to grow a mustache, but his mother asked him to cut it off. The women agree on everything else.

Marshall Ryan Maresca is a playwright, novelist, husband, father, and amateur chef who lives in Austin, Texas.

Michael Martone is the author of *Michael Martone*, a memoir in contributor's notes like this one.

Natalie McNabb lives and writes in Newcastle, Washington. She enjoys skiing, mountain biking, and double short Americanos with extra cream and secure lids.

David Miller is an American writer and senior editor of *Matador*. He and family live in El Bolsón, Patagonia. Visit him online at www.miller-david.com.

Sarah P. Miller is, in no particular order, a writer, a Wisconsin girl, a reader, a worrier, and a wife. All other details are unnecessary.

Ty Miller is a resident of McLean, Virginia, attending George Mason University.

John Minichillo lives and teaches in the Mid-South.

Gwendolyn Joyce Mintz is a fiction writer and poet. Unlikely 2.0 Press published her fiction chapbook *Mother Love*, available for download at www.unlikelystories.org/mintz0607.shtml.

Christoffer Molnar is a nice midwestern boy stuck in a mean East Coast town.

Madeline Mora-Summonte reads, writes, and breathes fiction in all its forms, from hint to novels. Visit her Web site at www.Madeline Mora-Summonte.com.

Rose Rappoport Moss, born in Johannesburg, now idles and writes novels, stories, and nonfiction in Cambridge, Massachusetts. Visit her at www.rosemosswriter.com.

Barry Napier has had more than twenty stories and poems published in print and online. He lives in Virginia with his wife and two children.

Brendan O'Brien enjoys exploring the big picture in blips and snippets. His fiction has appeared in several online literary journals. Visit him at www.huntnpeckhero.blogspot.com.

Joyce Carol Oates is the author most recently of the novel *Little Bird of Heaven*.

Daniel A. Olivas is the author of five books of fiction. His first full-length novel, *The Book of Want*, will be published in 2011.

Will Panzo is from Staten Island, New York.

Edith Pearlman's story collections include *Vaquita*, *Love Among the Greats*, and *How to Fall*. Her latest collection is *Binocular Vision*, published by Lookout Books.

Benjamin Percy is the author of a novel, *The Wilding*, and two books of stories, *Refresh, Refresh* and *The Language of Elk*.

Sophie Playle lives in England and works as an editorial assistant at Pearson Education. She has a degree in English literature with creative writing.

Jason Rice is one of the founders of Three GuysOneBook.com. He's written as Frank Bascombe for AICN, and his fiction has appeared in numerous literary magazines.

Samuel Rippey lives and writes in Rhode Island. He loves horror, fantasy, and dry martinis.

Katrina Robinson is a freelance writer from Aylett, Virginia. She received an English degree from the University of Virginia.

Jenifer Rosenberg is a freelance writer and creative geek based in New York.

Jess Row is the author of *The Train to Lo Wu*. He teaches at the College of New Jersey.

Robin Rozanski lives in Minneapolis. Her writing has appeared in the *Cypress Dome*, *Pindeldyboz*, and the *Humanist*.

Kathleen A. Ryan is a retired twenty-one-year veteran of the Suffolk County Police Department and a breast cancer survivor who lives on Long Island.

Marcus Sakey is, according to the *Chicago Tribune*, "the new reigning prince of crime fiction."

Sadly, his wife refuses to refer to him as His Highness.

Joe Schreiber lives in Hershey, Pennsylvania, with his family. He is the author of *No Doors, No Windows* and *Star Wars: Death Troopers*.

Jessa Slade burned through most of her words writing her debut urban fantasy romance *Seduced by Shadows* (NAL Signet Eclipse, October 2009). Visit her at www.jessaslade.com.

Noel Sloboda lives in Pennsylvania, where he serves as dramaturge for the Harrisburg Shakespeare Festival and teaches at Penn State York.

Andrea Slye writes horror and urban fantasy from her home in the Pacific Northwest, where dark skies and gray clouds are the best inspiration.

Kelly Spitzer's fiction has appeared in *Story-glossia*, *Keyhole*, *Redivider*, *Cream City Review*, *Hobart*, *Vestal Review*, and other publications. Visit her at www.kellyspitzer.com.

Agnieszka Stachura's work has appeared in *Tiny Lights*, the *Funny Times*, *swink*, *Ghoti*, and *Passages North*. She does not smoke.

J. J. Steinfeld has published nine short story collections, a poetry collection, and two novels, most recently *Word Burials* (Crossing Borders Enigmatic Ink).

Peter Straub is the author of eighteen novels and two collections of shorter fiction. He has won eight Stokers and two World Fantasy Awards.

Jake Thomas is currently struggling with his MFA in screenwriting at Chapman University. That's it.

Bob Thurber is an old, unschooled, multi-award-winning writer living in Massachusetts. Visit his Web site at www.bobthurber.net.

Jade Walker is the overnight editor at Yahoo! News. She's also the writer behind the *Blog of Death*, *New Hampshire News*, and the *Starting Point*.

Ben White lives in San Antonio, Texas, with his beautiful wife and edits *Nanoism*, a publication for Twitter-sized fiction.

Amber Whitley currently resides in Cincinnati, Ohio, with her husband, three "loving" cats, and assorted Soviet Union paraphernalia.

Sue Williams is an assistant editor at *Narrative*. Her fiction appears in numerous magazines, including *Narrative*, *Night Train*, and *Salamander*. Visit her at www.suewilliams.co.uk.

F. Paul Wilson is an award-winning, *New York Times* bestselling novelist best known as creator of the urban mercenary Repairman Jack. Visit him at http://www.repairmanjack.com.

Robley Wilson's longer work includes five story collections and three novels, the most recent of which is *The World Still Melting*. He lives in Orlando.

Mercedes M. Yardley writes whimsical horror. Swing by www.abrokenlaptop.wordpress.com.

Mabel Yu is a writer from the Washington, D.C., area. Her work has appeared in *Cream City Review*, *Inkwell*, *Quick Fiction*, and *Quarter After Eight*.

J. Matthew Zoss is a freelance video game critic, blogger, and fiction writer who spends far too much time in front of the computer.